Young Learner's

Y-517

My Favourite Stories

AF540059

Old Lady and the Butterflies

The Greedy Mouse

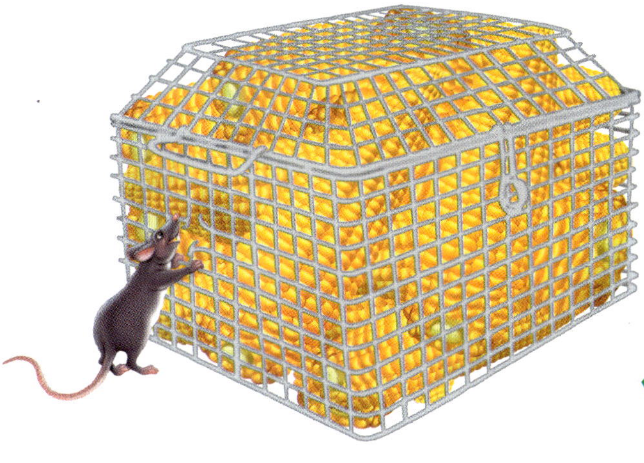

Old Lady and the Butterflies

A long time ago, an old lady lived alone in a little cottage by the river. A cobbled path lead to her cottage. Beautiful flowers grew on either side of the path.

In a small village nearby, lived many fishermen. They often visited the old lady and gifted her with fish. The old lady would, in return, give them flowers from her garden.

The villagers knew that the cottage was a blessed one. At night, the cottage glowed under the starlit sky. Fishermen would often see a beautiful young girl and some dwarfs singing and tending the garden. They would disappear with the first light of dawn.

Amongst the humble fishermen there was a rich and proud couple. They were rude to everyone. They never visited the old lady, and never even greeted her when they passed by her cottage. They wanted the flowers from her garden, but were too proud to seek the old lady's permission.

One evening, as the old lady sat knitting by the window, the fisherman couple stealthily entered her garden and began plucking the flowers.
The old lady came out of her cottage and scolded them, “You may take as many flowers as you want, but you should have taken my permission.”

“Oh, what an ugly old woman she is!” the woman said to her husband.

“We shall pluck as many flowers as we want. We don’t need her permission! She is too old to cause us any harm,” the man said to his wife and they continued plucking the flowers.

The old lady was very angry now. She ordered them to leave her garden immediately. But the man laughed at her saying, "My pretty wife wants these flowers and we shall leave only after taking as many flowers as she wants. Stop us if you can!"

The old woman said, "I let everyone take flowers from my garden, but you both need to be taught a lesson for being so rude and stealing my flowers."

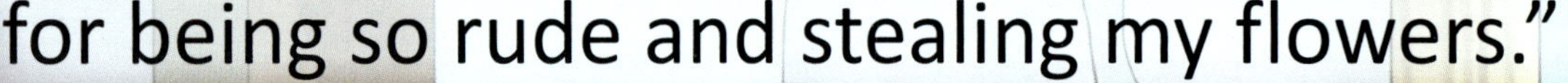

The old lady waved her hands in the air and cast a magic spell, "You seem to love these flowers a lot, so let me turn you both into butterflies so that you may always be near these flowers."

The proud couple turned into butterflies and to this day they can be seen hovering around flowers. The couple paid a heavy price for their arrogance.

Moral: Pride comes before a fall.

The Greedy Mouse

A little mouse was very hungry. He looked here and there but could find nothing to eat. Suddenly, he came upon a basket full of ripe golden corn. His mouth began to water. He looked for an opening in the basket but there was none.

The basket was made of strong steel wire and he was unable to cut the wires with his teeth. Then, he saw a gap in the wires of the basket. With great effort, he managed to squeeze through the tiny gap.

He entered the basket and began to eat the delicious juicy corn. He thought to himself, “I am so lucky to have found this corn. Now, I shall have a feast!” He ate as much as he could and when he could eat no more, he decided to get out of the basket.

He tried to wiggle through the gap but could not do so. He got stuck in the gap as he had become very fat!
He began crying loudly and calling for help.

A rabbit heard his cries and came up to him. He said to the mouse, “My little friend, I can pull you out of the basket but you have to share the corn with me. Pass me a few grains of corn, and then I shall pull you out.” However, the greedy mouse did not want to share the corn with anyone. He asked the rabbit to go away.

The rabbit went away and the mouse started shouting for help again. A cat who was hiding behind a haystack, heard the mouse and the rabbit. Her mouth began to water when she saw the fat mouse. She had an idea. She went up to the mouse and offered her help.

The mouse got scared upon seeing the cat and quickly hid in the corn pile.

The clever cat called out, “Dear mouse, do not be scared. I don’t want the corn. I don’t even eat mice anymore. Come, give me your hand, and I shall pull you out.”
The foolish mouse believed her. He let the cat pull him out of the basket. The cat held him by the tail and laughed out loud, “How silly you are! I love eating fat mice.” The mouse pleaded for mercy but the cat did not let him go. She gobbled him up in one big bite. The cat had a hearty meal and the mouse lost his life because of his greed.

Moral: There is no greater disaster than greed.